for Papa

"Mother! I hear a noise!"

# I HEAR A NOISE

## DIANE GOODE

DUTTON CHILDREN'S BOOKS    NEW YORK

Library of Congress number 87-3060
ISBN 0-525-44884-5

Published in the United States by Dutton Children's Books,
a division of Penguin Books USA Inc.
375 Hudson Street, New York, New York 10014

Editor: Ann Durell    Designer: Riki Levinson

Printed in Hong Kong by South China Printing Co.
First Unicorn Edition 1992
10 9 8 7 6 5 4 3 2 1

"It's only the wind. Now go to sleep.
Good night."

"MOTHER!  I hear it again!"

"It's just a branch against the window.
Sleep tight."

"MOTHER!"

"Oh my!"

"We're home!"

"What have you got there?"

"None of your business!"

"MOTHER!"

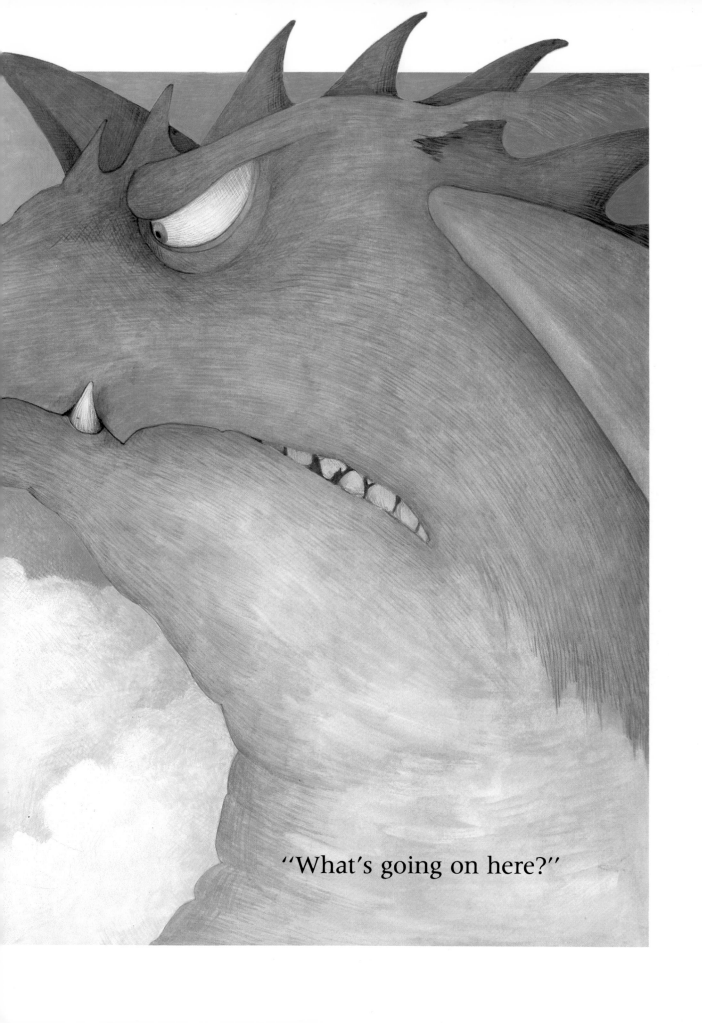

"What's going on here?"

"You should all be ashamed."

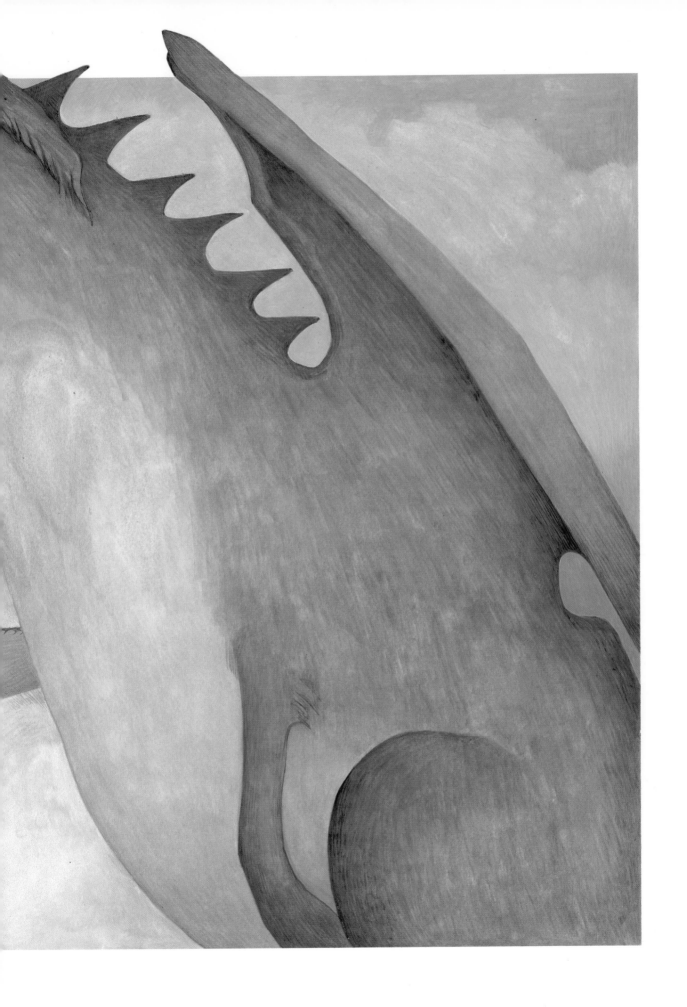

"I want you to take them right
back where you found them . . .
and don't ever touch them again."

"Good night."

"Sleep tight."